TROPICAL FISH

Color & Story Album

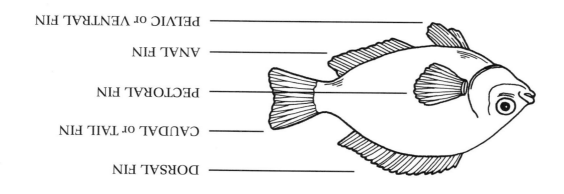

DORSAL FIN

CAUDAL or TAIL FIN

PECTORAL FIN

ANAL FIN

PELVIC or VENTRAL FIN

Written by Malcolm Whyte
Illustrated by Andrea Tachiera

Contributing Consultant: Thomas F. Ihde
Education Department, John G. Shedd Aquarium

TROUBADOR PRESS
an imprint of
PRICE STERN SLOAN
Los Angeles

Text copyright © 1995 Word Play, Inc.
Illustrations copyright © 1995 Andrea Tachiera
Published by Troubador Press, an imprint of Price Stern Sloan, Inc.,
A member of The Putnam & Grosset Group, New York, New York.
Printed in the United States of America. Published simultaneously in Canada.

ISBN 0-8431-3875-0

3 5 7 9 10 8 6 4 2

ANEMONEFISH
(Pomacentridae)

ℐNTRODUCTION

Beneath the ocean's glittering surface an endless population of tropical fish weaves through the tunnels and towers of coral reefs. The variety of fish is immense and wondrous, their colors brilliant.

Each chapter presents a different family of these diverse creatures. Fish from the same family, but different parts of the world, are pictured together. The text describes individual species' locales along with common and scientific names, sizes, coloring, and other identifying characteristics.

We hope these pages lead to a greater understanding and enjoyment of these marine marvels the next time you visit them in an aquarium or in the freedom of the open water.

Clown Anemone Fish / Percula Clown Fish
(Amphiprion percula)
Range: Tropical Indo-Pacific • Length: 3 inches (7.5 cm)

There are 26 known species of these remarkable fish that live in and around poisonous sea anemones for protection. They are unaffected by the anemone's stinging tentacles because of a special mucous layer on their skin. The tentacles offer a safe refuge for the fish while the anemones may absorb food particles dropped by the fish. This type of relationship, where both species benefit organically, is called symbiosis.

Percula clown fish are the smallest and best known of the genus. Their colors range from orange to brown, with wide white bands, and black-banded fins crisply bordered with white.

ANGELFISH
(Pomacanthidae)

Imperial Angelfish

(Pomacanthus imperator)
Range: Indo-Pacific • Length: 14 inches (36 cm)

Like a number of other angelfish, the imperial angelfish changes color dramatically as it grows to adulthood. While the young body (top, far left) shows mostly dark blue to black with white and blue bands, the adult body (top, center) turns to a dark blue-green decorated with yellow-to-orange stripes, and yellow caudal fin (tail). Its eye stripe, throat, and shoulder bands are black edged with blue.

Regal Angelfish

(Pygoplites diacanthus)
Range: Indo-Pacific and Red Sea • Length: 10 inches (25 cm)

All Angelfish live in pairs, mate for life, and are very aggressive to other fish. This colorful variety is brilliant orange on top merging to yellow below, and striped with pale blue bands bordered in black (center, right). Its ventral and caudal fins are yellow, the dorsal fin (top of body) is blue, and the anal fin (near the posterior opening) is yellow with light blue stripes.

Blue-Girdled Angelfish

(Euxiphipops navarchus)
Range: Indo-Pacific; Australian Archipelago • Length: 8 inches (20 cm)

Rich blue spots shower a saddle of deep yellow running down to a solid blue belly. Light blue spots lead to a bright yellow tail outlined in blue. Blue lips, yellow throat, and a gold ring around the eye make this fish (middle, left) a treat to discover under the sea.

Blue King Angelfish

(Pomacanthus annularis)
Range: Indo-Pacific Coasts • Length: 16 inches (40 cm)

Several blue stripes lay over gleaming gold scales on the adult blue king (bottom). Its pectoral fin is yellow with a blue band at the base, the caudal fin is yellow-white with an orange tip, and it sports a distinctive gold spot ringed with light blue high above its eye.

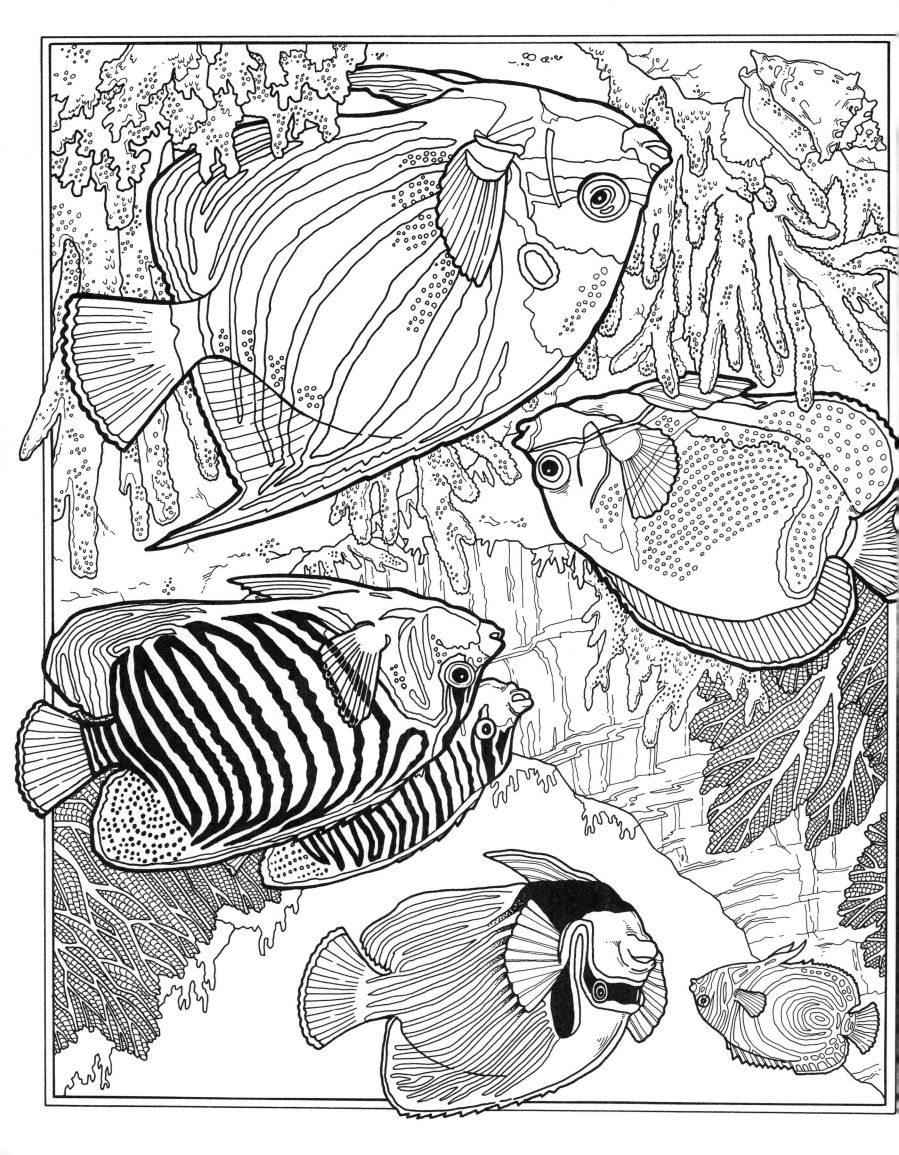

BATFISH
(Ephippidae)

Round-Faced Batfish

(Platax tiera)
Range: Indo-Pacific • Length: 24 inches (61 cm)

Extended dorsal and anal fins make the adult batfish (far left) look like one large swimming fin. It cruises coastal areas where the salty sea sometimes meets with such fresh water as rivers to create a brackish mix. The round-faced batfish has an extended, yellow-edged ventral fin resembling a goatee. Wide silvery stripes run vertically down its brown body, fins, and face, emphasizing the "flying wing" shape of this unusual looking tropical fish.

Long-Finned Batfish / Seabat

(Platax pinnatus)
Range: Indo-Pacific • Length: 30 inches (76 cm)

Young batfish (bottom) are flat, small, and thin. To a would-be predator they can look just like a dead leaf drifting in the water and not worth going after as a meal. A cheery red-orange fringe encloses this batfish. Wide, vertical, ivory stripes cross its brown-to-black body; a thinner stripe runs vertically just behind its eye. The seabat can be found off the coast of East Africa and the Red Sea to the East Indies, Australia, and the Philippines.

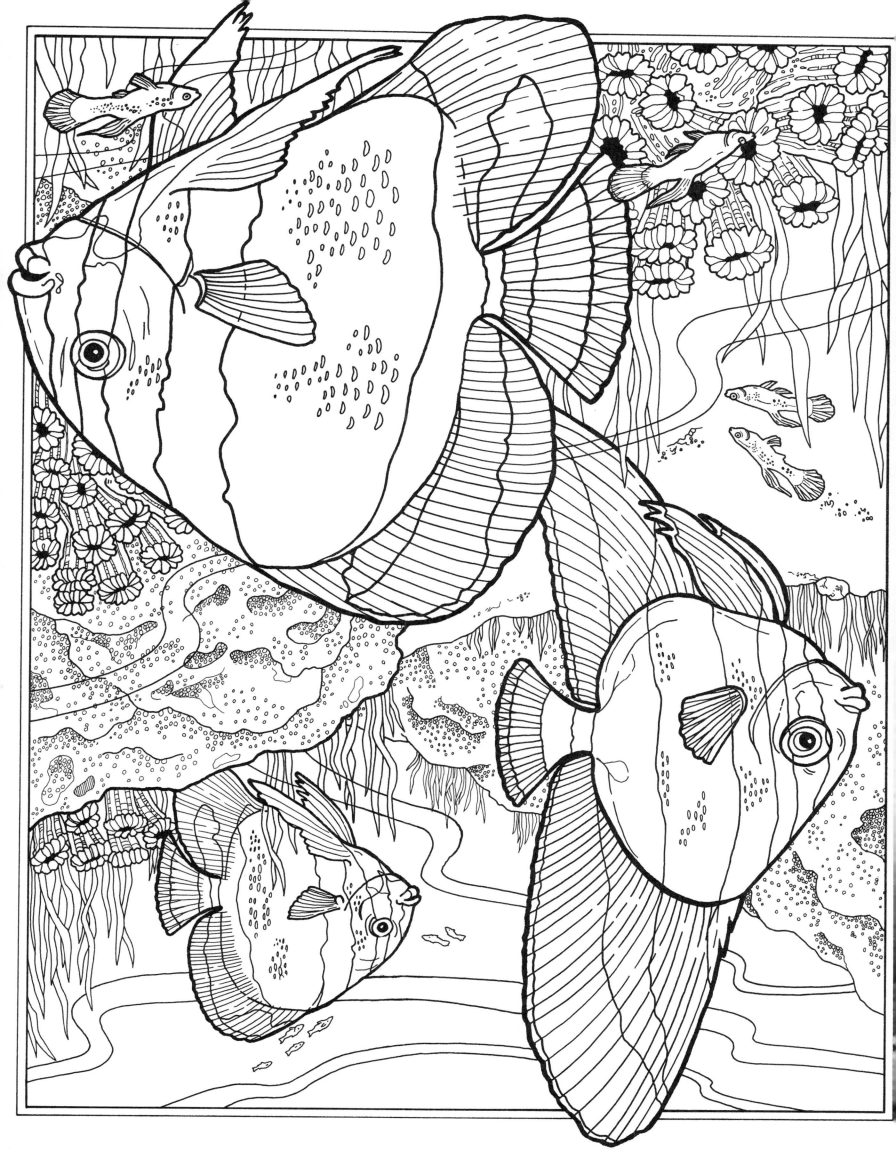

BUTTERFLYFISH
(Chaetodontidae)

Copperband Butterflyfish / Beaked Coralfish

(Chelmon rostratus)
Range: Tropical Indo-Pacific • Length: 8 inches (20 cm)

With bristlelike teeth, butterflyfish neatly nip off coral polyps (a protruding hollow mass) for food. This flashy silver and gold-striped beaked variety (top) is especially equipped to dig out small crustaceans in narrow coral crevices with its protruding mouth. Beaked coralfish have a notable white-ringed "eyespot" on their dorsal fins and black bands around their caudal fins.

Saddleback Butterflyfish

(Chaetodon ephippium)
Range: Indo-Pacific • Length 12 inches (30 cm)

Rather than blending in with their background as some fish do, the boldly marked butterflyfish protects itself with an aggressive nature and by staying very close to shelter. The saddleback (middle, left), for instance, has a gleaming silver-blue or orange body trimmed with a blue-rimmed orange tail, orange chin, and a dashing black eye band. The large black "saddle" on its back is edged with white in front and red-orange behind.

Threadfin Butterflyfish

(Chaetodon auriga)
Range: Tropical Indo-Pacific • Length: 9 inches (23 cm)

Butterflyfish slip easily through very small coral crevices for food and shelter with their flat, thin bodies. The strong, smooth coloring of the threadfin (bottom) emphasizes the streamlined look: Its front half is silvery white, while the back half is yellow-gold, diagonally divided and accented with darker diagonal lines. A black mask hides its eyes behind a purple, projecting mouth, and a distinctive black "eyespot" tops off its dorsal fin.

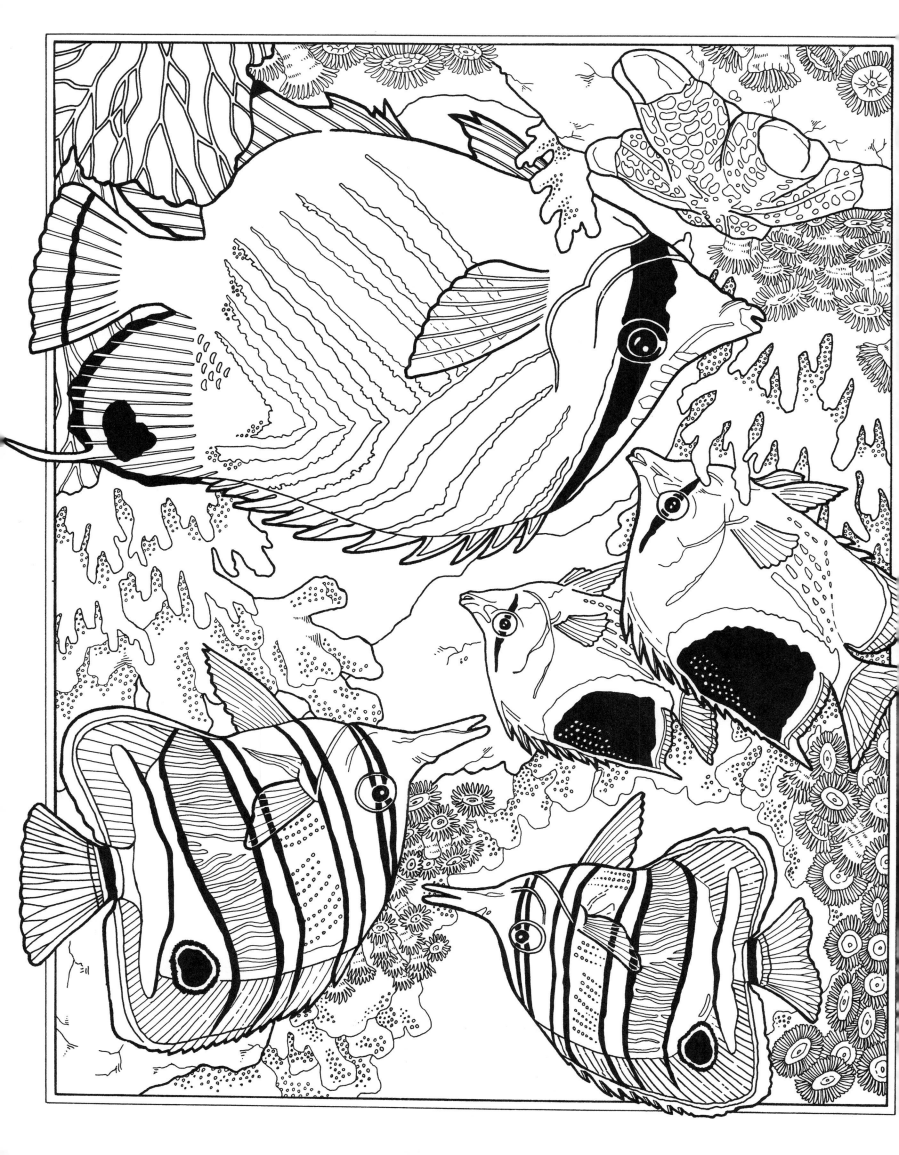

GROUPERS
(Serranidae)

Panther Grouper

(Chromileptes altivelis)
Range: Indian Ocean to Western Pacific • Length: 20 inches (50 cm)

Of the 400 species of groupers—from the four-inch (10 cm) anthias to the eight-foot (2.5 m), 700 pound (315 kg) jewfish—the panther grouper (top) is on the small side, but one of the most striking. A variety of black dots pattern its silvery-gray fins and sandy-colored body.

Coral Rockcod / Red Grouper

(Cephalopholis miniatus)
Range: Tropical Indo-Pacific • Length: 18 inches (45 cm)

Groupers are bottom dwellers. Lying in wait in crevices or on the rocky bottom they attack their prey from undercover with their large mouth and powerful teeth. As beautiful as it is strong, the red grouper (bottom) is well named. Its body is scarlet above, fading to a lighter ruby on the sides. Small black-edged blue spots cover the fish and luminous blue borders the rear fins.

GRUNTS & DRUMS
(Pomadasyidae & Sciaenidae)

Porkfish

(Anisotremus virginicus)
Range: Tropical Western Atlantic • Length: 12 inches (30 cm)

The colorful members of the grunt family, porkfishes (top) are decorated with gold and silvery-blue bands from gill cover to caudal fin. Their fins and nose are golden-yellow. Two deep brown bands, separated by a blue-white collar, run down the head. Grunts are named for the loud noise they make by grinding their powerful throat teeth together. Their swim bladder amplifies the sound.

Jackknife Fish

(Equetus lanceolatus)
Range: Tropical Western Atlantic; Caribbean Sea • Length: 9 inches (23 cm)

Another noisy group known as drum fish (bottom), produce a variety of sounds by vibrating muscles against the swim bladder; sort of like twanging a rubber band against a balloon. Snappily dressed in grayish-tan, the jackknife fish sports three white-edged, deep brown bands, one of which covers an area from its knifelike dorsal fin to the tip of its caudal fin.

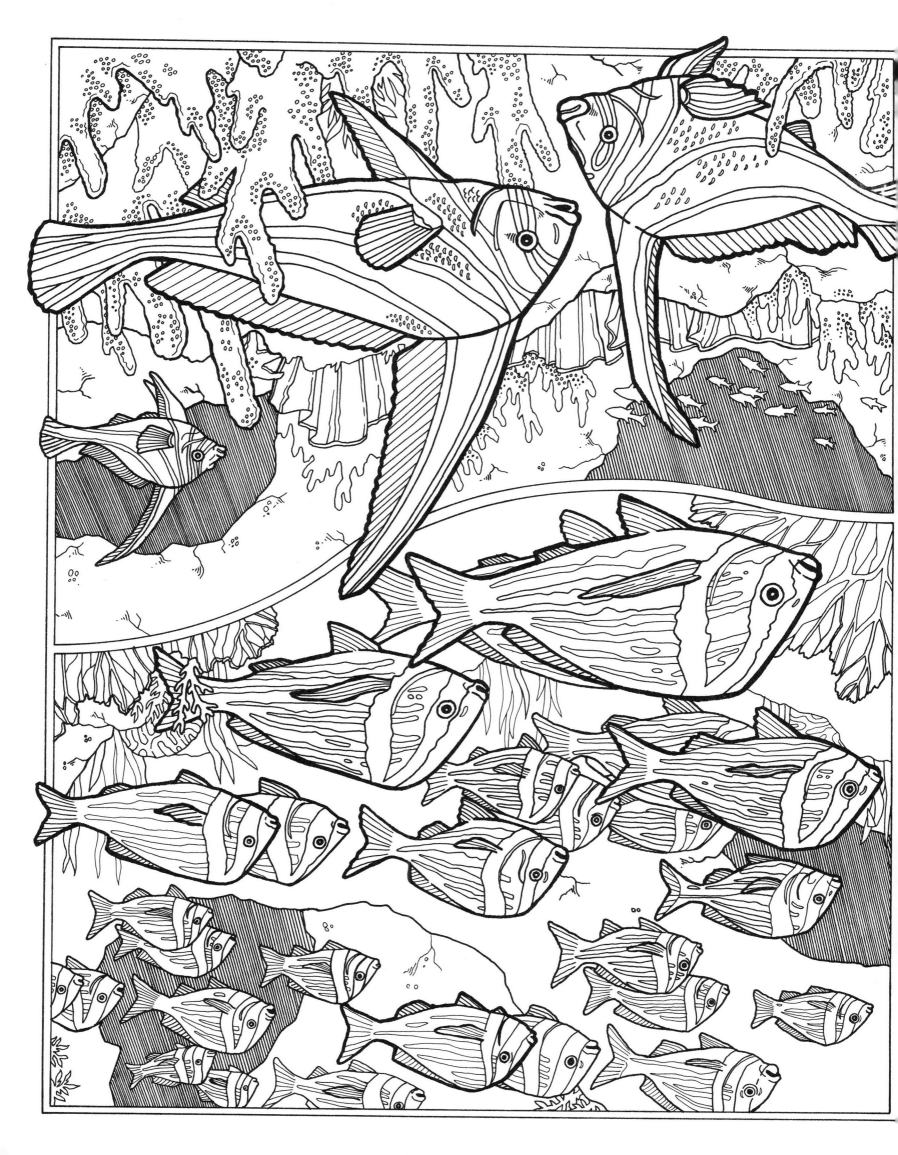

MORAYS
(Muraenidae)

Zebra Moray

(Echidna zebra)
Range: Tropical Indo-Pacific and Red Sea • length: 50 inches (127 cm)

Morays inhabit all warm seas, especially the shallow areas of tropical waters. Although they look fierce they are timid creatures that rarely move from their burrows in the protective coral or rocks. As distinct as the zebra moray's markings are—midnight black body interspersed with white rings (far left)—the colors also blend in with its dark coral, rock, and sand surroundings, protecting it from predators.

Snowflake Moray

(Echidna nebulosa)
Range: Tropical Indo-Pacific and Red Sea • Length: 36 inches(92 cm)

The speckled color of the snowflake moray (right, top and bottom) cleverly hides it in the varied texture and colors of its territory. Two rows of black, starlike spots run from head to tail along its ivory-to-tan colored body. Smaller, cream-colored dots sprinkle the larger spots. Most active at night, morays hunt small fishes, mollusks, and crustaceans that they devour with rows of strong, grinding teeth.

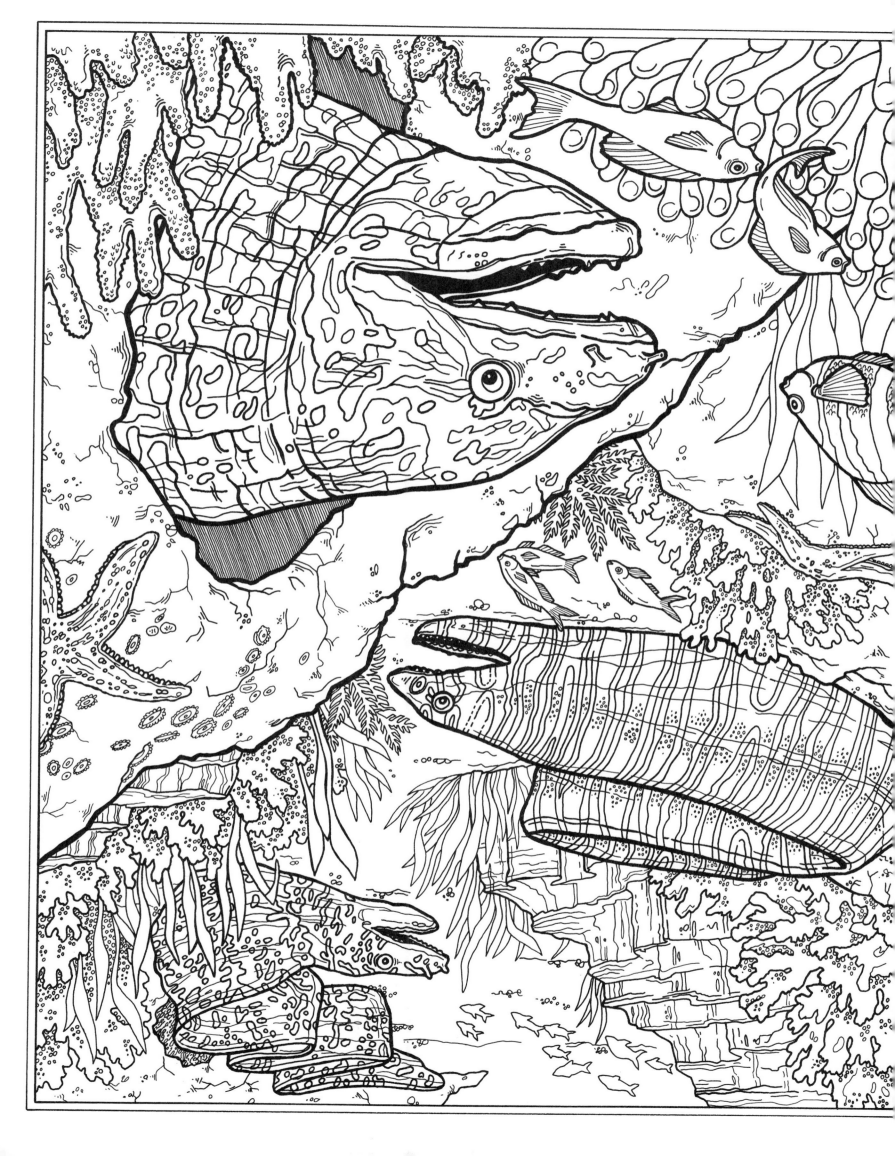

Parrot Fish
(Scaridae)

Blue-Barred
Orange Parrot Fish
(Scarus ghobban)
Range: Pacific and Indian Oceans • Length: 36 inches (91 cm)

Like the jungle birds, parrot fish have vivid, splashy colors and sharp, rounded beaks. Their jaws consist of solid plates of teeth that have grown together, well designed to scrape up algae and nip off branches of coral for their herbivorous (feeding on plants) diet. Like their near relatives the wrasses (also featured in this book), the parrot fish's colors change from the juvenile to adult and from the female to male forms.

The adult male blue-barred has an iridescent blue-green body with highlights of pink and yellow, deep turquoise fins with pink centers, pink lips and blue bands under its chin. At night it sleeps in the rocks on the ocean floor in a cozy nest made from strands of its own mucous. The female's coloring, as in many fish species, is low key for protection.

RABBITFISH
(Siganidae)

Reticulated Rabbitfish / Vermiculated Spinefoot

(Siganus vermiculatus)
Range: Indo-Pacific • Length: 15 inches (38 cm)

Rabbitfish have a smooth, softly curved face like a rabbit, and like their furry namesake, they are herbivorous. They are related to surgeon fish (also featured in this book) but lack that breed's tail "scalpel." The spines in the rabbitfish's fins, however, are very sharp and can be harmful. A blue-to-brown, mazelike pattern runs over the fish's tan body. Alternating brown and tan rays grace its dorsal and ventral fins, and brown spots splash over this lively swimmer's tail.

SEA HORSES
(Syngnathidae)

Australian Fringed Sea Horse

(Phyllopteryx foliatus)
Range: Australian Ocean • Length: 10 inches (25 cm)

Sea horses, like their relatives the pipefish and trumpet fish, have tubelike snouts and long, thin bodies. Unlike the pipefish, though, the sea horse's body curls up at the end, specifically to anchor itself to coral and sea plants. They swim "standing up" rather than lying lengthwise in the water as most fish do. A brisk fanning of their dorsal and pectoral fins moves them among the reefs. Pale green, leafy-looking fins and bony spines disguise the Australian sea horse (top) perfectly when hiding in the slow waving seaweeds.

Oceanic Sea Horse

(Hippocampus kuda)
Range: Indo-Pacific • Length: 12 inches (30 cm)

Male sea horses give birth to the young. The female lays 200 to 300 eggs through a tube into a pouch on the male's front where he carries them until they hatch. A maximum of only 55 eggs in the brood will hatch in about 45 days. From the moment they are born the young swim freely and independently. All sea horses are greenish-gray to tan in color but can blend with the background when danger strikes. The oceanic sea horse (bottom) is among the largest of these fanciful fish.

SCORPION FISH
(Scorpaenidae)

Lionfish / Red Firefish / Dragon Fish / Turkeyfish
(Pterois volitans)
Range: Indo-Pacific • Length: 15 inches (38 cm)

Scorpion fish are the only bottom feeders found in every sea. Their showy colors serve as a warning to other fish, yet also help to hide them in their habitat. White-bordered, dark red and black stripes wildly decorate the lionfish's brownish-red head and body (top). Its soft dorsal, anal, and caudal fins display rows of handsome dark brown or black spots. But don't let the gay colors fool you. This fish has poisonous spines that can be very harmful to humans.

Zebra Lionfish
(Dendrochirus zebra)
Range: Indo-Pacific • Length: 7 inches (18 cm)

The elegant, fanlike pectoral fins of the zebra lionfish (bottom) blaze with alternating rays of red and brown, highlighted by bright white spots. Brown and white dot the other fins, too. Light red and white bands cross its rose red body, and larger orange-red spots cover its head. The scorpion fish lives alone rather than in a school, and lurks among reefs and rocks, waiting to snap a passing meal into its big, broad mouth.

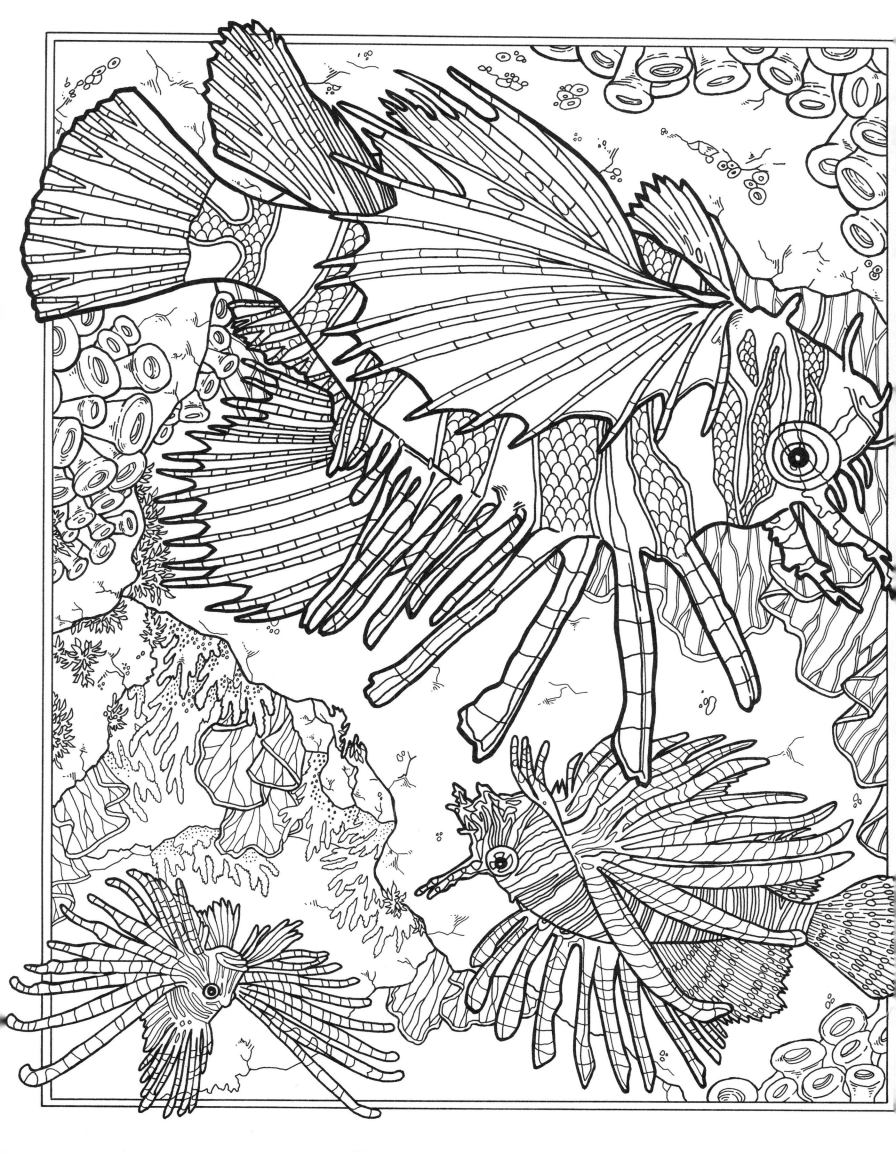

Surgeon Fish or Tangs
(Acanthuridae)

Pacific Sailfin Tang
(Zebrasoma veliferum)
Range: Indo-Pacific and Red Sea • Length: 16 inches (40 cm)

This vegetarian fish (top) grazes the shallows for algae and other plants where its tall dorsal fin sticks out of the water like a sail. Vivid, curved, white and blue bands, bordered with orange, cover its body from dorsal to anal fins. Its spotted tail echoes the pattern of ivory dots that sparkle on its head.

Powder-Blue Tang
(Acanthurus leucosternon)
Range: Indian Ocean • Length: 6 -3/4 inches (17 cm)

Beautiful and dangerous: that's the surgeon fish. Also called tang or doctor fish, surgeon fish are named for the scalpellike spine located on both sides just in front of the tail. Like a switch blade, the spine springs out from its flat sheath, and with it pointed forward the fish can take a side swipe at another fish—even another surgeon fish—to protect its territory. Often just a flick of the surgeon fish's tail will warn off an intruder.

With its rich blue body, powder blue–framed black face, yellow pectoral and dorsal fins, and sky-blue anal, pelvic, and caudal fins, the powder blue tang (bottom) wins a beauty prize. Humans, however, should be wary of the sharp "doctor's knife" when handling the fish.

TRIGGERFISH
(Balistidae)

Undulate Triggerfish

(Balistapus undulatus)
Range: Tropical Indo-Pacific to South Africa • Length: 12 inches (31 cm)

Dazzling yellow-orange lines play over this triggerfish's olive green-to-blue body, from its mouth to shiny gold tail (top). Distinctive orange lines streak around its mouth and yellow freckles dot its nose. Typical of triggerfish, its eyes sit well back on its body to protect them from the sharp spines of its favorite meal, the sea urchin.

Picasso Fish / Painted Triggerfish

(Rhinecanthus aculeatus)
Range: Indo-Pacific • Length: 12 inches (31 cm)

With a wonderfully abstract design, this fish looks as though Pablo Picasso, the famous artist, painted it (far left). A long yellow line trails back from its blue and yellow lips to meet yellow, white, and green bars running down through its eyes. White, brown, and green diagonals stripe its silvery body in back. Three black dotted lines finish off its tail.

Clown Triggerfish

(Balistoides conspicillum)
Range: Indo-Pacific • Length: 20 inches (50 cm)

The dorsal fin of the triggerfish rises up and locks into place. This unique feature serves two purposes: it creates a sharp, nasty mouthful for a would-be predator, and it can hold the fish firmly into a reef's crevice for protection.

The make-up of the aptly named clown triggerfish (bottom) runs from bright yellow-orange lips to large, chalk-white spots on its black belly. Its black trigger sticks out of a yellow saddle on its blue-black back, the rear dorsal and anal fins are striped orange, white, and yellow, and its black caudal fin flashes with a jolly yellow band.

Trunkfish & Porcupinefish
(Ostraciidae & Diodontidae)

Spotted Boxfish

(Ostracion meleagris meleagris)
Range: Indo-Pacific • Length: 6-1/4 inches (16 cm)

Trunkfish and boxfish all sport a boxlike, bony armor that has holes for eyes, mouth, fins and anus. These fish are slow swimmers, and some, like the spotted boxfish (top), release poison through their skin that is toxic to other fish. Color changes between juvenile and adult stages, and varies between male and female trunkfish. Dark blue-black bodies sprinkled all over with bright white spots mark the juvenile and female forms. The adult male stands out with his deep-black back dotted with white, while the rest of his brilliant blue body is covered with black-ringed yellow spots. A bold yellow stripe runs from his eye to his tail and a bright yellow-orange spot blushes his cheek.

Spiny Puffer / Balloonfish

(Diodon holocanthus)
Range: Worldwide Tropical Seas • Length: 20 inches (51 cm)

Porcupine fish, or puffers (bottom), surprise attacking predators by swelling up to three times their normal size. Swallowing great gulps of water, they become too big a mouthful for their attackers. When removed from water they inflate like a balloon with large gasps of air. This fish's sharp spines add to its defenses. Dark brown bars run through its eyes, and several large brown spots highlight its sandy-gold body.

WRASSES
(Labridae)

Bluehead Wrasse

(Thalassoma bifasciatum)
Range: Caribbean Sea; Tropical Atlantic • Length: 6 inches (15 cm)

Among the 600 species of wrasses in the world, many make ideal aquarium fish because of their beauty and size. In the bluehead (top), striking color changes occur. The juvenile and female forms are light greenish-yellow. The male, however, matures with a deep greenish-blue head, followed by bands of black and olive-green. Its yellow-green body ends in a black-lined caudal fin centered with pale green. Male wrasses build the brood's nest and watch over the eggs until they hatch.

Lyretail Wrasse / Moon Wrasse

(Thalassoma lunare)
Range: Tropical Indo-Pacific and Red Sea • Length: 9-3/4 inches (25 cm)

Jewellike reddish spots fleck the moon wrasse's elegant green body, one of the prettiest in this family of fish (bottom). Violet stripes curve around its green head, red scores the bottom of its dorsal and anal fins, and blue-violet borders its graceful yellow tail. A small, protruding mouth encloses the powerful teeth of the moon wrasse for cracking open crabs and mollusks that teem in the tropical seas.

IMAGINATIVE
COLOR & STORY ALBUMS
FROM TROUBADOR PRESS

All About Horses

Ballet

Cats & Kittens

Cowboys

Dogs & Puppies

Dolls

The Enchanted Forest

The Enchanted Kingdom

Exotic Animals

Giants & Goblins

The Great Whales

Horse Lovers

Hot Rod

Mother Goose

North American Indians

North American Sealife

Northwest Coast Indians

Tropical Fish

Unicorn

Wonderful World of Horses

Also look for our Troubador Funbooks, ColorPops, *and punch-out and assemble* Action *and* Play Sets.

Troubador Press books are available wherever books are sold or can be ordered directly from the publisher.
Customer Service Department, 390 Murray Hill Parkway, East Rutherford, NJ 07073

TROUBADOR PRESS
an imprint of
PRICE STERN SLOAN
Los Angeles